E
FIT
   Fitzpatrick, Marie-Louise.
      I'm a tiger too!

I'm a Tiger Too!

For
Diarmuid, Donnchadh
and Cian, with love,
with thanks to
Findabhair and Rousseau
for the inspiration

A NEAL PORTER BOOK

Copyright © 2001 by Marie-Louise Fitzpatrick

Published by Roaring Brook Press
A division of The Millbrook Press, 2 Old New Milford Road, Brookfield, Connecticut 06804
First published in the United Kingdom by Gullane Children's Books, London

Library of Congress Cataloging-in-Publication Data
Fitzpatrick, Marie-Louise
I'm a tiger too! / Marie-Louise Fitzpatrick.—1st American ed.
p.   cm.
Summary: A boy tries to play imaginative games with a cat, a dog, and a fish, but he
does not find a cooperative playmate until he meets another boy.
[1. Play—Fiction. 2. Imagination—Fiction. 3. Animals—Fiction. 4. Stories in rhyme.] I. Title.
PZ8.3.F63575 Im 2002
[E]—dc21   2001019396

ISBN 0-7613-1498-9 (trade edition)
0-7613-2410-0 (library binding)

Printed in China

10 9 8 7 6 5 4 3 2 1
First American edition

20983

I'm a Tiger Too!

Marie-Louise Fitzpatrick

ROARING BROOK PRESS
Brookfield, Connecticut

"Hey, Mew!

Are you a tiger?

I'm a tiger too.

Let's be tigers together.

nd tumble through the jungle.

Rrroarr!

Oh, don't go!

I don't want to be a tiger all alone.

Hey, Ruff, are you a wolf?

I'm a wolf like you.

We are wolves,
big and fierce.
Let's howl at the moon.

Woooooo!

Oh, don't go!

I don't want to be a wolf all alone.

Swish, swish, Mr. Fish, you and me,

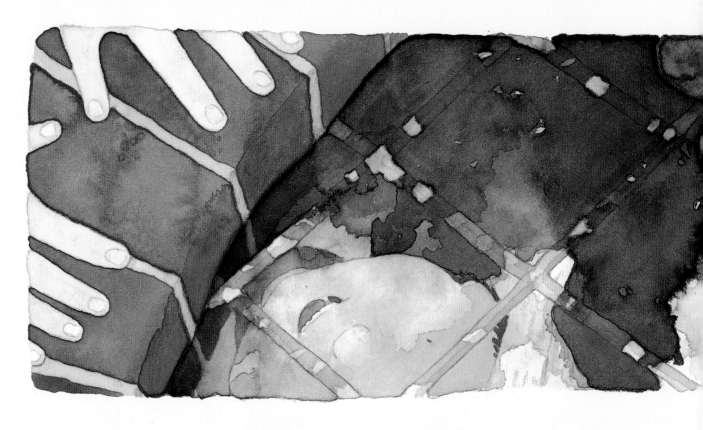

let's be sailors on the sea.

Over the waves, across the sea.
Swish, swish!

Oh, don't go!

I don't want to be a sailor all alone."

"What's going on?   Who are you?"

"I'm a boy," said the boy.   "I'm a boy like you."

"But I'm a tiger!" said
Tiger-Wolf-Sailor on the Sea.

"Will you be a tiger too?"

"I'll be a tiger," said the boy.

"Then we'll be tigers two."

Rrroar!